E
VAU   VAUGHAN, MARCIA K
       WOMBAT STEW

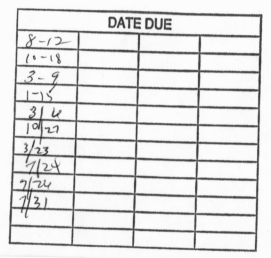

DATE DUE			
8-12			
10-18			
3-9			
1-15			
3/4			
10/27			
3/23			
7/24			
7-24			
7/31			

WOMBAT · STEW ·

Marcia K. Vaughan

Illustrated by
Pamela Lofts

Silver Burdett Press
Englewood Cliffs, New Jersey

For Mum and Dad with love.

Text © 1984 by Marcia Vaughan.

First published in 1984 by Ashton Scholastic Pty Limited (Inc. in NSW),
PO Box 579, Gosford 2250. Also in Brisbane, Melbourne, Adelaide, Perth and
Auckland, NZ.

Published in the United States in 1986 by
Silver Burdett Press, Englewood Cliffs, New Jersey.
ISBN 0-382-09211-2
Library of Congress Catalog Card No. 85-63492

Printed in Hong Kong

One day, on the banks of a billabong,
a very clever dingo caught a wombat . . .

and decided to make . . .

Wombat stew,
Wombat stew,
Gooey, brewy,
Yummy, chewy,
Wombat stew!

Platypus came ambling up the bank.

"Good day, Dingo," he said,
snapping his bill.
"What is all that water for?"

"I'm brewing up a gooey, chewy stew
with that fat wombat,"
replied Dingo, with a
toothy grin.

"If you ask me," said Platypus,
"the best thing for a gooey stew
is mud. Big blops of billabong mud."

"Blops of mud?" Dingo laughed.
"What a good idea.
Righto, in they go!"

So Platypus scooped up big blops
of mud with his tail and
tipped them into the billycan.

Around the bubbling billy,
Dingo danced and sang . . .

"Wombat stew,
Wombat stew,
Gooey brewy,
Yummy, chewy,
Wombat stew!"

Waltzing out from the shade
of the ironbarks came Emu.
She arched her graceful neck
over the brew.

"Oh ho, Dingo," she fluttered.
"What have we here?"

"Gooey, chewy wombat stew,"
boasted Dingo.

"If only it were a bit more chewy," she sighed. "But don't worry. A few feathers will set it right."

"Feathers?" Dingo smiled. "That would be chewy!" Righto, in they go!"

So into the gooey brew Emu dropped her finest feathers.

Around
    and around
the bubbling billy,
Dingo danced and sang . . .

"Wombat stew,
Wombat stew,
Crunchy, munchy,
For my lunchy,
Wombat stew!"

Old Blue Tongue the Lizard came sliding off his sun-soaked stone.

"*Sss*illy Dingo," he hissed. "There a[r]e no flies*ss* in this *sss*tew. Can't be wombat *sss*tew without crunchy flies*ss* in it." And he stuck out his bright blue tongue.

"There's a lot to be said for flies,"
agreed Dingo, rubbing his paws together.

"Righto, in they go!"

So Lizard snapped one hundred flies
from the air with his long tongue
and flipped them into the gooey,
chewy stew.

Around
   and around
      and around
the bubbling billy,
Dingo danced and sang . . .

"Wombat stew,
Wombat stew,
Crunchy, munchy,
For my lunchy,
Wombat stew!"

Up through the red dust popped Echidna.

"Wait a bit. Not so fast," he bristled,
shaking the red dust from his quills.
"Now, I've been listening to all this
advice — and, take it from me,
for a munchy stew you need
slugs and bugs
and creepy crawlies."

Dingo wagged his tail. "Why, I should
have thought of that.
Righto, in they go!"

So Echidna dug up all sorts of creepy crawlies and dropped them into the gooey, chewy, crunchy stew.

The very clever Dingo stirred
and stirred, all the while singing . . .

"Wombat stew,
Wombat stew,
Hot and spicy,
Oh so nicey,
Wombat stew!"

Just then the sleepy-eyed Koala climbed down the scribbly gumtree.

"Look here," he yawned, "any bush cook knows you can't make a spicy stew without gumnuts."

"Leave it to a koala to think of gumnuts," Dingo laughed and licked his whiskers.

"Righto, in they go!"

And into the gooey, chewy, crunchy, munchy stew Koala shook lots and lots of gumnuts.

"Ah ha!" cried Dingo. "Now my stew is missing only one thing."

"What's that?" asked the animals.

"That fat wombat!"

"Wait!"

"Stop!"

"Hang on, Dingo! You can't put
that wombat into
the stew yet."

"Why not?"

"You haven't tasted it."

"Righto! I'll taste it!"

And that very clever dingo bent over the billy and took a great big slurp of stew.

"I'm poisoned!" he howled.
"You've all tricked me!"

And he dashed away
deep into the bush, never again
to sing . . .

"Wombat stew,
Wombat stew,
Gooey, brewy,
Yummy, chewy,
Wombat stew!"